D1261763

HARLEY BASIL
AND THE LOST PUP

Lena
Cannata
Patterson

Illustrated by
Penny
Weber

Kevin W W Blackley Books, LLC
Copyrighted Material
Harley Basil and the Lost Pup

Copyright © 2019 by Lena Cannata Patterson

All rights reserved. No part of this publication may be reproduced, stored in a retrieval system or transmitted, in any form or by any means—electronic, mechanical, photocopying, recording or otherwise—without prior written permission from the publisher, except for the inclusion of brief quotations in a review.

For information about this title or to order other books and/or electronic media, contact the publisher:

Kevin W W Blackley Books, LLC
280 East Treehaven Road
Buffalo, NY 14215

www.kevinblackley.com
kevin.blackley@gmail.com

Library of Congress Control Number 2017960469

ISBN 978-0-9960839-7-3

Cover and Interior Design: Kevin W W Blackley Books, LLC
Cover and Interior Illustrations: Penny Weber

Printed in the United States of America

For Bette, Vera, and London.
You girls are my proudest achievement.
XOXO

And for AP, for always encouraging me to pursue my dreams.
XOXO

I also thank everyone who helped make this book a success,
specifically my family and friends who supported me and helped
make this book possible.

I love you all and thank you from the bottom of my heart.

My name is Harley Basil, and I'm a Welsh corgi dog.
Every day, I try to save my family from the dangers of
this world—but they think I'm crazy.

You see, I protect Max and Olive and their parents from four major dangers: water, darkness, balloons, and flash photography. They say I'm weird. I say they don't understand how dangerous the world is!

It's hard work protecting them. So I like to take naps. Long, relaxing naps ... anywhere in the house, actually. Usually, right in the middle of the kitchen floor.

One day I heard them talking about how lazy I was. I knew I had to change their minds. I had to prove to them that I am a hero.

My family was packing to go on a vacation to England, and arranged for a dog-sitter to come visit me while they were gone. However, I knew this was going to be my chance.

The day my family was leaving, I put my plan into action. Everyone was rolling their luggage to the car, and I snuck out behind them. On the driveway, Max opened his large suitcase to pull out one of his books. When he turned to tuck it into his backpack, I jumped into his suitcase, diving under his clothes to hide, before he closed the lid again.

They were very surprised to see me when we arrived in London!

My family thought I was sleeping all day at the hotel.
But little did they know I had a plan.

Every day, on my own, I went to a new place: Big Ben, the River Thames, and many restaurants. And everywhere I went, I saw pictures of a lost puppy. Danger was lurking around every corner—I could see it. I asked other dogs to help me find the pup, but they had not seen her and were no help.

On the last day of the trip I knew time was running out. I had searched all around the city. The one place I hadn't looked yet was Buckingham Palace, where the queen lived. That day, my family decided to take me along with them to the palace.

A lot of people bunched together outside the big building's black-and-gold gate and fence, but I didn't give up. Olive walked me on the leash while I looked around and sniffed for clues.

Finally, I spotted a small dog by a fire hydrant. She looked like the lost puppy on the posters. That must be her. I zigzagged through the crowds, pulling Olive behind me.

I was so close to the lost pup when, out of nowhere—balloons attacked! I ran under them, but Olive got stuck in the strings. I had to use my teeth to free her.

After we escaped the clutches of the balloons, I looked up to see the puppy running toward the large water fountain in the middle of the square. This time I raced off, tugging the leash from Olive's hand—no time to waste!

When I got there, the puppy was gone. Max was sitting on the side of the fountain, throwing pennies into it. A Great Dane came by and jumped into the water, sending a big splash into the air, but I pushed Max out of the way just in time!

People had seen how I saved Max from the water, and they gathered around me to take my picture. I crouched in their shadows, scared by all the flashes from the cameras. Still, they kept pushing me back.

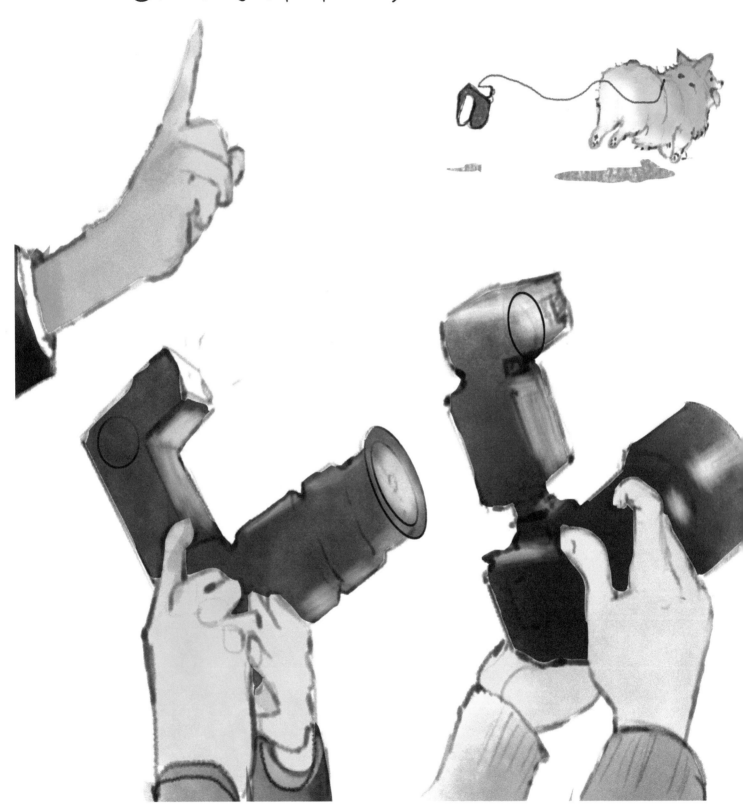

I ran away—away from the strangers and my family.

After a few minutes, I stopped at a curb to catch my breath. I had let the puppy get away from me, and now I was lost, too. I was all alone and very tired.

WHIMPER ...

Then I heard a sound ... a whimper. Like from a puppy. The little lost pup!

I looked around, trying to find where the sound was coming from. I followed my ears to the dark sewer grate in the street nearby. It was the puppy, and she was stuck under the sewer grate.

As I crept down to look, I saw it was dark and scary inside. I could see the puppy blinking her blue eyes at me. She needed my help. This was it, my chance to prove what a hero I was.

I took a deep breath, closed my eyes, and stuck my head in the dark opening.

The puppy was close enough for me to grab the scruff of her neck with my mouth. I slowly pulled the puppy out to safety, and she gave me a big wet lick to say thank-you.

A crowd of people had formed around the sewer grate by now, and everyone cheered. My family had found me just in time to see the rescue.

Max and Olive were smiling at me and clapping. I felt so happy that I had saved the puppy!

A palace guard was among the crowd too, and after seeing the rescue, he invited me to the palace.

When we arrived back at the front gate with the puppy, the guard was waiting there for us. The crowd parted, and we followed him through the open gate. Once the gate shut behind us, a trumpet began to play. The guard said this meant the queen was coming!

As the queen stepped out of her carriage, I nudged the little pup toward her, just as her other dogs ran into the courtyard to greet her.

The smiling queen hugged the little pup tight. Then she said she wanted to know how she could thank me. I thought for a moment and noticed a statue of a knight nearby.

I had been very brave that day. I needed something to show people what a protector I was, so I asked for a symbol of my bravery.

Later, I felt so proud as the queen knighted me "Sir Harley Basil." Now my family would finally understand my quirks and see that I was really a hero.

And that is how I, Harley Basil, the so-called quirky and lazy corgi, became Sir Harley Basil.

Photo credit: Ariel Hawkins Photography

Lena Cannata Patterson has wanted to write a children's book about her old dog, Harley Basil, for quite some time. As a child, she loved reading picture books, and even became a teacher when she grew up. This is her first book, but definitely not her last! When she's not chasing after her kids, she likes to throw parties, read, and travel to new places. She lives in Buffalo, New York, with her husband and three daughters. For more about Lena, visit www.lenapatterson.com.

Penny Weber is a full-time artist and illustrator from Long Island, New York, where she's lived all of her life. Penny attended classes at the School of Visual Arts in New York. She works both digitally and traditionally (in acrylics and watercolors). Over the years, she has created residential murals and greeting cards, and she still offers portraits, caricatures, and pet portraits to independent clients. Penny is proud to say that she has never missed a deadline.

In 2007, Penny turned her attention to children's book illustration and quickly signed with Wendy Mays and Janice Onken, to be represented by WendyLynn & Co. Since then, Penny has illustrated many books, including the Chris P. Bacon series for Hay House Publishers. Some of Penny's other clients are McGraw-Hill Education, Seed Learning, Tilbury House, and Learning A-Z.

She has a husband, three children, a cat, and she is heavily lobbying for a puppy.

ABOUT SIR HARLEY BASIL

The real Harley Basil was a good dog who lived to be fourteen years old. Although quirky and lazy, he was a great protector, loved naps, and could always be counted on to lick table scraps from dishes.

CPSIA information can be obtained
at www.ICGtesting.com
Printed in the USA
BVHW02*2104170418
513640BV00013B/47/P